JAN -:- 2011

CATCH THAT PASS!

THE #1
SPORTS SERIES
FOR KIDS

CATCH THAT PASS!

LITTLE, BROWN AND COMPANY
New York   Boston

Little, Brown and Company

Hachette Book Group
237 Park Avenue, New York, NY 10017
Visit our website at www.lb-kids.com

www.mattchristopher.com

Little, Brown and Company is a division of Hachette Book Group, Inc.
The Little, Brown name and logo are trademarks of Hachette Book Group, Inc.

First Paperback Edition: September 1989
Originally published in hardcover in August 1969 by Little, Brown and Company

The characters and events in this book are fictitious. Any similarity to real persons, living or dead, is coincidental and not intended by the author.

Matt Christopher® is a registered trademark of
Matt Christopher Royalties, Inc.

ISBN 978-0-316-13924-3

Library of Congress Control Number 77-77442

30 29 28 27 26 25

COM-MO

Printed in the United States of America

To
Helen L. Jones

CATCH THAT PASS!

Third and eight.

The pass down. The Cadets had to pass. They weren't gaining enough yardage on the ground.

Jim Nardi stationed himself in the middle linebacker slot in front of the Cadets' center. To his far left was Bill Brown, to his far right Yak Lee. The cornerbacks and safety men were spread wide in a parallel line behind them.

"Hup one! Hup two!" yelled Terry Jason, the Cadets' quarterback.

The snap from center. Jason faded back.

The Vulcan and Cadet lines tore into each other in a crash of helmets and shoulder pads.

Jim bolted through the narrow hole between right guard and center, then stopped. Jason had thrown a pass, and the ball was lobbing over Jim's head!

Jim leaped. His hands wrapped around the ball and brought it down. In the same instant, he saw a red-and-white helmet and blazing red jersey coming at him. The thick padded shoulders looked like the shoulders of an angry, charging bull.

Jim's nerves shattered like glass. Frantically he flung the ball to the ground.

Shreeeeep!

The whistle stopped the would-be tackler. Less than a yard from Jim, he grinned behind the double bars of his face mask.

"Why didn't you hang on to it?" he said. "I haven't had a tackle yet."

"I'm sorry," replied Jim. "Why don't you ask Terry to try it again?"

He spun on his heel and started back to his position when a hand grabbed his elbow. He looked into the angry eyes of Hook Wheeler, the left safety man.

"You had it in your mitts! Why'd you knock it down?"

Their eyes clashed. "It was slipping out of my hands," said Jim. Darn Hook! Why didn't he mind his own business?

"Slipping, my eye! You had it in your mitts! I saw you! Everybody did!"

The whistle shrilled. "Come on," snapped the ref. "Let's hustle it up."

Fourth down and eight. The ball was on the Cadets' twenty-seven-yard line. The Cadets went into punt formation. Their fullback kicked the ball — a long, spiraling aerial. Hook Wheeler caught it on the Vulcans' thirty-eight and carried it across the forty —

the middle of the Midget football field — to the Cadets' thirty-one.

The defense went out; the offense came in. Someone slapped Jim Nardi on the back. "No harm done, Jim. We got the ball anyway."

Jim looked at Bucky Hayes, the husky left tackle and Jim's close buddy. "It . . . oh, never mind." He wanted to tell Bucky, too, that the ball had slipped, but why lie about it? Why talk about it at all? He'd hang on to it the next time, if there was a next time.

He trotted up to the bench, avoiding Doug's eyes. Doug was his brother and coach of the Vulcans. He was in college and had played football his freshman year. In high school he had made All-State end.

"What happened out there, Jim?" he asked quietly.

"You mean when I —"

"When you knocked the ball down."

"Well, that's all. I knocked the ball down."

"But you had it in your hands."

Jim flushed. "No, I didn't! You don't think I'd knock it down if I —"

"Okay, okay. Forget it."

Chris Howe quarterbacked the Vulcans. He got the ball to the Cadets' nine-yard line. Then the Vulcans lost five yards on an off-side penalty. On the next play, Chris flipped a spiral pass into the end zone, hitting left end Ben Trainor a yard inside the out-of-bounds line for a touchdown. Fullback Ronnie Holmes kicked the conversion. Seven to nothing.

In the second quarter, a Cadet safety man picked off a pass Chris had intended for Pete Witz, the flashy right end. The Cadet was pulled down on the Vulcans' fourteen. They tried a double reverse and gained six yards. Jim Nardi made up his mind that no runner was going through the middle. He'd stop any man cold who would try.

"Hup one! Hup two!"

The quarterback faked a run through right tackle, drawing some of the players toward that side of the line. But the fullback had the ball! He was fading back behind the right side of his line. He was looking toward the coffin corner. And then he passed.

He was clever. Instead of throwing to the coffin corner, he threw to the right center of the end zone near the goalpost. Jim, breaking back away from the scrimmage line, sprang a couple of steps toward it, leaped, and caught the ball!

As he came down with it, he saw a bright red helmet with a white stripe through its middle. He saw the bulging shoulders of a blazing red jersey.

He got panicky. He didn't want to be hit. He was *afraid* to be hit.

He let the ball drop. The Cadet fell on it. So little time elapsed between the moment Jim caught the ball and dropped it that the call could've been either way — a completed pass or an incomplete pass.

Shreeeeep! went the whistle. "Incomplete pass!" yelled the ref.

Jim turned and almost bumped into Hook. "What's the matter, Nardi?" Hook snarled. "That's the second time you dropped the ball! I suppose it slipped through your hands this time, too."

2

Third and four.

The Cadets' tight seven-man line looked like a red wall facing the Vulcans. The Vulcan linebackers played up close, intent on plugging every possible hole. Only the two safety men played deep, watching for a forward pass.

The snap from center. Jason handed off to his fullback. The fullback cut toward right end. For a split second, Jim wondered: Was this another pass play?

It wasn't. The fullback plunged around

on
through
down. The men with
measured. A first down!

"Hold that line! Hold that line!" shouted the Vulcan fans.

"We want a touchdown! We want a touchdown!" chanted the Cadet fans.

First and goal to go. Four yards for a touchdown.

Terry barked signals. He took the snap, faded back a few steps, and passed. His left halfback caught it on the one-yard line and plunged over for the score. They tried the conversion and missed.

"See what happened?" Hook bellowed at Jim. "If you had held on to that ball, it would've still been seven-oh!"

Right safety man Dil Gorman tapped

ght," he
for guts!"

aw red, but this time it wasn't
the color of an opponent's jersey. It was
hot, flaming anger. He knotted his fists and
stepped toward Hook, ready to let him have
it. Then he stopped. No, he thought. No
matter how badly he wanted to make Hook
eat those words, he wasn't going to fight
here. He'd be thrown out of the game.
Maybe Hook would be thrown out, too. The
only thing to do — the best thing to do —
was to ignore the wise guy.

It was awful to admit that both Dil and
Hook were right. But they were. Every time
Jim tried to intercept a pass, he would see
an opponent come at him and that terrible
fear would sweep through him and rush to

10

his head and swell as if it were ready to explode. He had to get that feeling out of his system. He had to or he'd never play football in high school. Doug might not even let him keep playing with the Vulcans after this, their first game of the season.

Someone slapped him on the back. "Did you hear a time-out or something?" It was Bucky.

Jim forced a smile. "C'mon! Let's go!"

They lined up for the kickoff. The whistle shrilled. The Cadets' line sprang forward. The fullback booted the ball. It sailed end over end into Vulcan territory. Hook caught it on the twenty-two and bolted up the field, twisting and dodging.

"C'mon! Give me interference!" Hook shouted.

Jim Nardi fell in front of a Cadet, then got up and blocked another Cadet as he headed toward Hook. The block helped Hook gain another six yards. He was tackled on the Vulcans' thirty-four.

The defensive unit trotted off the field. The offense took over.

"What went on out there?" Doug asked when Jim reached the sideline.

"Nothing," said Jim.

"Did Hook or Dil say something to you?"

Jim unbuttoned the chin strap of his helmet and took the helmet off. The cool air refreshed his sweating head. "Okay. They made me sore. But I didn't do anything, did I? I didn't start a fight, did I?"

Doug looked at him hard. "No, Jim, and I'm glad you didn't. I'm darned glad."

Jim met Doug's eyes evenly. Doug was tall, close to six feet. His steel-blue eyes were steady. They had had their arguments, with Doug usually winning them. But afterwards, when Jim had a chance to think, he'd always agree that Doug was right. Like the time Doug had warned him about riding the bike with weak brakes. Jim had been too lazy to fix them and did so only after Doug had started to take the brakes apart himself.

The game went into the fourth quarter with the score still 7 to 6 in the Vulcans' favor. At the four-minute warning signal, the Vulcans had the ball on their own nineteen. Chris Howe faked a handoff to right halfback Ken Morris, who started to plow through right tackle. But it was fullback Ronnie Holmes who took the ball and galloped for eight yards through the left side of the line.

A wild scramble followed. And loud shouting. Ronnie had fumbled the ball. A red-jerseyed player began jumping up and down. The Cadets had recovered!

"Oh, no!" cried Jim.

"Get in there!" yelled Doug. "Hold them!"

Terry Jason flung a long pass on the first play. He hit his man perfectly, and the runner carried the ball to the Vulcans' eighteen before Hook nailed him.

"I think there's a magnet in that ball and another one in that receiver," observed Bucky Hayes. "No man can throw a pass that perfect."

"I hear he wears telescopic contact lenses," said Yak Lee, the right linebacker.

"That answers it," replied Bucky.

In two downs the Cadets moved the ball to the nine. Then Terry tried a quarterback sneak, but lost a yard.

Fourth down and two.

The Cadets called time.

"I've got a magnet at home," said Jim. "I'll bring it with me next time."

Dil Gorman looked at him. "A good idea," he said. "You should've thought of it sooner."

Jim flushed and looked away. He had really opened his trap at the wrong time then.

Time was up. The Cadets went into a huddle, then broke out of it and got into position at the line of scrimmage. Jim saw that Jason was standing back and that the fullback was a couple of yards behind him. They were going to try a field goal!

"Hup one! Hup two!"

Jason caught the snap and put it in position on the ground. Jim blasted through a narrow hole between center and right guard. He heard the sound of shoe meeting football and saw the pigskin sailing over his head.

A shout rose, and Jim knew that the ball had gone between the uprights. 9–7.

That was the final score, too.

3

The Porsche Carrera 6 sped down the straightaway, then zoomed around the turn and along the wall that was almost vertical. It cut sharply around the second curve, buzzed down the straightaway on the opposite side of the track, and passed the red Lotus 30 as the cars sped around the 45-degree bend and under the overpass.

Chuckie Gorman laughed. "I'm a lap ahead of you!"

Jim Nardi depressed the plunger of his controller all the way to the bottom for a split second, then quickly let up on it as the

Lotus 30 reached the curve on the left side of the track.

"Two more laps to go," he said after a quick glance at the counter. "Guess you'll win this race."

"Well, I have more experience than you have," Chuckie said, sitting forward in his wheelchair with a wide grin on his face. "You know what I'm going to be when I get out of this chair, don't you?"

"What?"

"A race driver!"

Click!

"There's the counter!" cried Chuckie. "Ten laps! Want to race again?"

"Sure. Why not?"

They stopped their cars. Jim lifted them off the track and placed them on the starting line. The track was on a platform in Chuckie's room. It had two lanes, a grandstand, pit stops, mechanics, spectators, and

17

trees and shrubbery that made it look real except for its being miniature.

Model car racing was Chuckie's favorite sport. He was always calling up Jim to come over and race with him. Of course Chuckie's brother Dil raced with him, too. And so did Hook Wheeler. But of all the guys, Chuckie liked Jim the best, and Jim liked him.

Chuckie had become crippled from a car accident when he was five. He was sure that someday he was going to get out of that wheelchair and walk. And maybe he would. He did exercises every afternoon at the clinic, and his muscles seemed to be getting stronger.

They had just started the race when someone came into the room. Jim glanced over his shoulder, and all at once his spirit melted like butter on hot pancakes.

"Hi, Dil," he said. "Hi, Hook."

The boys greeted him and then exchanged greetings with Chuckie. Jim jiggled the plunger up and down with his thumb to slow down the Lotus 30 as it completed its first lap and headed for the first sharp curve. Chuckie's Porsche Carrera 6 was only a foot or so ahead of his Lotus.

"Who's winning?" asked Hook.

"We've just started our second race," replied Chuckie. "I won the first one."

"That's nothing to brag about," said Dil. "Maybe you've got Jim shook up."

"Sure, that's why you beat him," Hook joined in. "Jim doesn't like contact. He might've been afraid you'd crash into him."

"Will you guys pipe down?" cried Chuckie irritably. "Who can race with you guys shootin' off your mouths?"

The controller was hot in Jim's hand. Weren't those guys ever going to get over his dropping those passes yesterday? Darn 'em, anyway.

The little red car twisted around the curve at the right, shot up the wall and then along the short straightaway, its tail wagging as if it were trying to shake something off. Chuckie's Porsche Carrera 6 came speeding up behind it, gulping up a big gain on the straight.

The Lotus 30 looked fuzzy as it headed for the overpass. Jim blinked to clear away the fuzz. He was thinking of Dil and Hook watching them, of what they had said about him, and of the terrible feeling that had come over him just after he had intercepted the passes. The controller was hot, and he was sweating. Man, that terrible feeling. He could remember it as if it had happened only a little while ago.

The Lotus 30 tore through the overpass and up the short straightaway to the curve. It was going fast. *Too* fast!

Jim let up on the plunger. But too late. The car jumped the track. It crashed against the white fence, tore loose a post, zoomed over the edge of the platform, and plunged to the floor.

Jim stood paralyzed. A long minute passed before he could unglue his feet from the floor. Then he went and picked up the car. The front axle had broken loose from the chassis. The front end of the car was split open. And the windshield had come off.

4

Don't worry about it, Jim," said Chuckie. "I can fix it."

Jim wiped the sweat from his upper lip. "No, I'll take the pieces home. It was my fault. I'll fix it."

Chuckie glared at Dil and Hook. "It was you guys' fault!" he cried. "You kept shooting off your mouths!"

"We're sorry, Chuckie," Dil apologized. "We really didn't mean anything by it."

"Sure," said Hook. "We were just kiddin'. Are you sure you can fix it, Jim? You got tools?"

"My dad has tools," replied Jim quietly. He was holding the car body in one hand, the pieces in the other. "I'll bring it back as soon as I finish it, Chuckie."

"Take my tube of epoxy," offered Chuckie. "It's good to cement stuff." He wheeled around to the left side of the track, lifted a yellow tube off one of the shelves on the wall, and handed it to Jim.

"Thanks, Chuckie," said Jim.

No one said a word as he walked out.

He thought about football all the time he worked on the model racing car in the garage. He knew the big reason why Dil and Hook were on his back. They were sure that the Vulcans would've won the game yesterday if he had hung on to those intercepted passes. Well, maybe they would've and maybe not. So what? Was it a crime to have lost? It was only a game. And their first one, at that.

Darn! He was only looking for an excuse! Of course the game would've turned out differently if he had hung on to those passes. But he'd been scared — scared stiff of being tackled and getting hurt. He had tried to do something about it, hadn't he? He had tried not to be scared. But he had failed. That scary feeling just grabbed him like electrified steel fingers.

Somebody came in. It was his little sister, Karen. Her hands were tucked up inside the sleeves of her green sweater. "Isn't it cold in here?" she said. "Brrrrr!"

"I turned on the electric heater," answered Jim. The heater was on the bench beside the tools, warmth pouring from the twin circles of coils.

Karen came forward and stood in front of it. "Whose car's that?"

"Chuckie's. I was racing it and it jumped the track and landed on the floor."

He had cemented the split front end together and was putting the axle back in place.

"I just saw Hook leaving the Gormans'," said Karen. "Was he there when you were?"

"Yeah."

"He's a worm," she said.

"Aw . . ."

"Aw, what?"

"Aw, nothing."

"Aw, nothing, my eye. You know what you should've done when he yelled at you? You should've socked him one."

"Yeah. And get kicked out of the game. Oh, sure."

"*I* wouldn't have cared. I mean I wouldn't have cared if I'd been in your place and he'd yelled at me and I'd socked him and got kicked out of the game. After all, anybody can miss a pass."

Jim looked at his sister. Man, it was a good

thing Hook wasn't here. She looked mad enough to follow through with everything she said. "Karen, you don't understand."

She glared at him. "I don't understand? Just because you're older than I am and I'm a girl, you think I don't understand?"

"Look, I had the ball. I'd already caught it. I got scared and dropped it when I saw the tackler coming at me. You just don't know how I felt —" He swallowed hard and turned her around to face the door. "Look, leave me alone, will you? Go into the house. Maybe you can help Mom with something."

She spun and looked at him hotly. "You mean you admitted it to that . . . that worm that he was right and you were wrong?"

Jim shrugged. "I didn't admit anything. But he was right, Karen. I do get scared, and I can't help it. Don't you see? I just can't help it!"

Her voice softened. "Does Doug know?"

"I — I think so."

"Don't you think he can help?"

"How could he? I'm the one playing out there. I'm the one who gets the chance to intercept a pass."

"Why don't you ask Doug to let you play quarterback? Or halfback?"

Jim shook his head. "I'm not going to ask him anything. I don't want the guys to think that just because the coach is my brother I'm asking for favors. Anyway, Doug knows his stuff. He wants to develop Chris Howe in the quarterback position so that Chris will be broken in when he gets into high school."

"Don't you care about playing football in high school?"

"Sure, I do."

"Then why doesn't Doug put you some-where else?"

"Because he thinks he could make me a good middle linebacker, that's why! For crying out loud, Karen! Please don't bother me anymore, will you? I — I just don't want to talk about it anymore."

He finished repairing the model car, turned off the heater, and went into the house, taking the car with him. In his room he touched it up with paint and put it on a shelf to dry.

On Monday there was football practice after school, and Doug had the team scrimmage. Bill Clark, Doug's assistant coach, worked with the defensive unit and Doug with the offensive. After a few routine one-on-one plays, in which each defensive man covered his offensive man, Coach Clark suggested a new tactic.

"Let's try red-dogging 'em," he said. "You

linebackers break through the line and grab the ballcarrier before he has a chance to do anything. Okay?"

The teams lined up at the line of scrimmage. Chris Howe, quarterbacking for the offensive team, called signals. The ball was snapped. There was the thudding sound of helmets striking helmets, shoulder pads brushing shoulder pads.

Jim Nardi bulldozed through the narrow gap between center and right tackle. At the same time, he spotted right halfback Ken Morris taking the pitchout from Chris and starting to sprint toward left end. Jim's rubber cleats dug into the turf as he wedged through the line after the fast-running back. He caught up with Ken and tackled him a yard behind the scrimmage line.

Coach Clark grinned when Jim returned

to the defense's huddle. "Nice work, Jim," he said. "I think Doug'll have a man on you the next time."

Three plays later, Bill Clark had the linebackers red-dog again. This time a man blocked Jim two yards beyond the line of scrimmage. Chris fumbled the ball in his hurry to back away from the other plunging linemen and linebackers, and it was recovered by Marv Wallace, the right tackle.

Coach Clark kept the defensive unit in a huddle until the offense broke out of theirs. "I'm trying to make 'em think we're changing our pattern," he explained in a voice that wasn't supposed to carry beyond the U-shaped huddle. "But let's try the red dog again. It's working pretty good!"

Chris Howe barked signals. He took the snap, rushed back, faked a handoff to Ken Morris, then flipped a short pass over the line of scrimmage. Jim, charging through the line, saw the ball sail in his direction in a slow, crazy wobble. He stopped, leaped, and caught it. Just as his feet touched the ground, he saw Roger Lacey, the chunky right guard, rise from his knees and dive at him.

He was unprotected and had no time to move. Nothing was going to stop Roger from tackling him, tackling him *hard*. At that instant he was gripped with fear. His head got fire-hot. Roger's shoulder struck him just above the knees, and he went down like a chunk of lead. His shoulders and head struck the ground. Stars flickered and he clamped his eyes shut. From a distance he heard a whistle. He felt a weight lift from his legs. He looked up and saw Roger's grinning face.

"You okay?" asked Roger.

"Yeah," he answered automatically. He didn't know whether he was or not.

He started to get up and saw Ronnie Holmes, the fullback, grinning at him too.

"Hi, Jim," he said. "Look what I found." He was holding the football.

5

After supper Jim took the Lotus 30 back to Chuckie. The paint had dried, and the car looked brand-new.

"Looks great," said Chuckie, smiling. "Thanks, Jim. Want to race awhile?"

"No, thanks, Chuckie. I have homework to do."

"How are you feeling?" asked Chuckie.

"I feel fine. Why?"

"Dil said you got hurt practicing football. He said you might quit."

Jim's face colored. "I didn't get hurt. And I'm not going to quit."

A warm smile spread over Chuckie's face. "That's what I told him, Jim. I said you wouldn't quit. I said that you and I were a lot alike. You won't quit football and I won't quit trying to walk. Heck, Jim, what fun is it if we don't try? You've got to try, you know it?"

If there ever was a guy who could buck up a fellow, it was Chuckie Gorman.

Jim tried to keep Chuckie's encouraging words in mind during the game against the Astrojets the next day. But it wasn't always easy.

"You'd better check your pants," said Bucky Hayes to left end Ben Trainor. "I think you've got both legs in one pant-leg. You were running too much in one spot."

"Listen to roadrunner here," replied Ben,

buckling his chin strap as he got into the huddle.

"Pipe down and listen," said Hook Wheeler, the right safety man and captain of the defensive unit. "They're on our seventeen-yard line and might want to try another pass. Let's red-dog 'em."

They broke out of the huddle and hurried to the line of scrimmage. The ground was a little soft, but the game was too young yet for either team to have gotten their uniforms soiled. Only Tom Willis, the Astrojets' quarterback, had smudged his shoulder, spoiling the neatness of his black and white uniform.

"Seventeen! Thirty-two! Hike! Hike! Hike!"
The ball was snapped. Jim charged. He zipped past Bucky, who was trying to push his man aside, and saw the start of a criss-cross play. The two halfbacks were running

toward the middle where they'd meet Willis, from whom one of them would take the ball. Jim sprinted to reach the quarterback ahead of the halfbacks.

An Astrojet fell in front of him. Jim leaped. At the same time, he saw the right halfback take the handoff and scissor toward the left side of the line. Jim reached out for him, hoping to grab the guy's shoulder. The halfback looked his way, and Jim's fingers circled the top bar of the face mask. The guy's head jerked, and Jim let go. But it was too late. The whistle shrilled.

Jim stopped dead and stared at the ref. The ref was showing the foul: grabbing the face mask.

"Boy, you pulled a good one then!" Hook stormed. "A fifteen-yard penalty puts them on our two!"

"I can count," said Jim lamely.

Bucky slapped him on the back. "Forget it and let's hold 'em."

Jim glanced at Hook, anxious to redeem himself. "Hook, let's red-dog 'em again."

Hook frowned, thinking hard. "Okay," he agreed. "Red dog!"

They blasted through the line like fearless commandos and broke up Tom Willis's quarterback sneak. The ref placed the ball on the four-yard line. It was second and goal.

Willis took the snap and faded back. The red dog wasn't on now. Jim, breaking toward the line, cut back sharply as he saw the fullback swing around right end and buttonhook in behind the line of scrimmage. Willis passed just as Jim moved. The ball came floating through the air. Jim caught it on the run, bolted toward the left side of the line, and ran as he had never run before. No one was near him.

Seconds later he crossed the goal line for the touchdown. Bucky was the first to jump on him for the team hug. From the stands the Vulcan fans were whooping it up.

Hook kicked the conversion. Seven to nothing.

Hook Wheeler kicked off. The Astrojets' left safety man caught the ball on the twenty-two, and Marv Wallace brought him down on the twenty-eight.

"Seventy-eight yards!" Bucky grinned at Jim. "You ran like a scared jackrabbit along that sideline!"

"I wasn't going to let anybody get me," said Jim, smiling. Boy, scoring that touchdown at the crucial moment made him feel great. That ought to shut up Dil and Hook for a while. Chuckie Gorman had seen it, too. He was sitting near the stands among the other Vulcan fans.

"Nineteen! Thirty-four! Twenty-one! Hike! Hike! Hike!"

Tom Willis faded back, then handed off to his fullback, and the guy plowed through left tackle for four yards. On the next play, Marv Wallace got too anxious and was off-side before the ball was snapped. The five-yard penalty put the ball on the Astrojets' thirty-seven.

Second and one.

Willis bucked for two yards and a first down.

A double reverse gave the Astrojets five more yards. They were moving. A red dog on the next play held them to a two-yard gain. Then the fullback took a pitchout and raced down the right sideline. Left end Ben

Trainor chased after him. The runner tried to stiff-arm Ben and crept closer to the white line. He took two steps out of bounds. Then Ben nailed him.

Shreeeeek! The ref stood on the spot inside the boundary line where the runner had stepped out of bounds and signaled the personal foul sign.

Ben sprang to his feet and stared at him. "Personal foul?" he shouted. "Why?"

"For tackling him out of bounds," explained the ref. He stepped off fifteen yards and placed the ball on the sixteen. "First and ten!" he yelled.

The Astrojets lost two yards on a line buck, and a whistle shrilled, announcing the end of the first quarter. The teams exchanged goals, and the ball was put on the Vulcans' eighteen.

Second and twelve.

Tom Willis barked signals. The ball was snapped. Willis faked a handoff to his left halfback, then faded back. Jim pushed aside a blocker on his way after the quarterback, but stopped on a dime as he saw Willis pull back his arm and wing a pass. The ball was a high looping spiral to his left side, and intended for a receiver buttonhooking in. The receiver was running between Jim and the ball. He was about to catch it when Jim leaped and batted it down.

"Way to go, Jim!" yelled Bucky Hayes.

"My eye. He could've caught it."

Jim turned. Dil Gorman was walking away, kicking the sod with his heels. Jim looked back at the spot where he had knocked down the ball. There had been no one in front of him, no one near him except the intended receiver. Yes, he could've intercepted the pass. Could've made a good gain. And it would've been the Vulcans' ball.

Ronnie Holmes came in. Jim went out.

"No one was near you that time," said Doug coldly. "You could've run a long way. Maybe all the way."

Jim's heart pounded. "I didn't think," he said.

"You weren't scared of being tackled?"

Jim stared at him. His pulse raced. "No." So Doug knew. He had probably known all along.

A roar burst from the Astrojet fans. Jim saw a player in a black-and-white uniform in a corner of the Vulcans' end zone. He had tossed the football up into the air and was jumping madly, as if he had just scored a touchdown. Which he had.

They tried the conversion, and missed.

Jim chewed his lips. "I suppose you won't let me go in again."

"Sure, I will," replied Doug. "Something tells me that you need to play until you get that feeling knocked out of you, one way or another."

7

Jim went in during the four-minute time period. The Astrojets had the ball on their thirty-eight. It was second and eight.

So Doug knew about me, Jim thought. Yet he hasn't bawled me out. He really wasn't mad at me when he told me I'll play until that feeling gets knocked out of me. I guess I don't understand my own brother.

The Astrojets tried an off-tackle play and picked up a first down.

"We better stop 'em," said Hook, "or we'll blow that seven to six lead."

The Astrojets pulled a surprise pass on the

first down that took them to the Vulcans' eighteen. It was an eleven-yard gain and another first down. A line buck and then a double reverse got them six more. Then they tried a pass. It was a wobbly one, falling far short of the intended receiver. Hook Wheeler pulled it down, dodged an Astrojet tackle, and sprinted down the sideline for thirty-four yards before he was bumped out of bounds.

The offense took over, but they couldn't get the ball past the Astrojets' ten-yard line before the first half ended.

The Vulcans kicked off to start the second half. The kick was poor. The ball hit the ground on the forty-yard line and bounced to the thirty, where an Astrojet scooped it up and carried it back to the Vulcans' thirty-eight. Jim hit him there like a tank.

"What a funny one you are," Hook said to Jim, cracking a grin, a sight almost as rare as hen's teeth. "You tackle like nobody's business. But when you have the ball, you're scared stiff of somebody tackling *you*. I can't figure it."

Jim shrugged. "I'll get over it."

"You think so?"

Jim started away. "I think so," he said over his shoulder.

The teams formed at the line of scrimmage. Tom Willis barked signals. Jim shifted back and forth in the middle linebacker slot, anxious to burst through and haul down the ballcarrier. Hook was right. He wasn't afraid to tackle. As a matter of fact he *enjoyed* it.

The snap from center. Jim tore through the line. Amid the loud noise of shouts and of helmets thudding against helmets and shoulder pads, Jim heard a shrill sound. But he was springing forward. And suddenly he was falling on Tom Willis, falling on him hard.

Phreeeeep!

Jim rolled off Tom and looked up at the ref, who was crouched above him, finger pointed at him like the tip of a sword. "Fifteen yards! Didn't you hear the whistle?"

Jim stared. "No! What did I do?"

"You were piling on, son."

"Oh man, oh man!" cried Hook, stamping his feet.

The ref picked up the ball, stepped off fifteen yards from where the violation took place, and spotted the ball on the Vulcans' twenty-six.

"Jim," said Bucky Hayes, "how do you get the knack of always doing the wrong thing at the wrong time?"

"Guess I'm just plain lucky," Jim answered, then frowned in bewilderment. "But I still don't know what happened, Bucky!"

"You don't? Willis had fumbled the ball.

48

And then you jumped on him. That's what happened, man."

First and ten. The Astrojets tried an end-around run and picked up two. Then the fullback found a hole through right tackle and gained seven.

"They need a yard for a first down," said Bucky. "Think they'll try a sneak?"

"Who knows?" said Hook.

It was a forward pass to their left end. And it was a good one. Their end caught the ball on the run and went over easily for their second touchdown.

"Guess they pulled a sneak, all right," said Bucky sourly. "A sneaky pass."

"Yeah," grumbled Hook.

This time the kick was good. Astrojets 13, Vulcans 7.

The third quarter ended with the Vulcans in possession of the ball on their own eighteen.

Fourth quarter. Chris Howe faded back to pass but couldn't find a receiver and was tackled on the twelve.

"Move out there, Pete!" yelled Doug. "Buttonhook!"

Second and sixteen.

Chris faded back again. This time Pete buttonhooked in behind the scrimmage line, but his guard closed in on him like a hawk. Chris heaved the ball. It spiraled through the air toward the left sideline. Left halfback Mike Ritter grabbed it out of the air and streaked to the Astrojets' twenty-three before he was pulled down.

The Vulcan fans roared. Bucky drummed on Mike's helmet excitedly.

"Beautiful!" said Doug.

Chris took the snap, faked a handoff to Mike, then faded back. He looked for a receiver. Every eligible man was covered.

"Uh-oh," mumbled Bucky. "He's going to get creamed."

An Astrojet tackle went after the quarterback. Chris dodged him and started to run toward the right side of the line. Right guard Roger Lacey blocked his man. Ronnie Holmes threw a block on the Astrojet end, clearing the way for Chris. Chris crossed the twenty . . . the fifteen . . . and was tackled on the twelve. It was another first down.

"That's my boy!" yelled Bucky.

Jim smiled. "Thought he was going to get creamed?"

The snap. Chris faked a handoff to Mike, then gave the ball to Ronnie. The fullback plowed through the right tackle for two yards. They tried a buck through the left side and gained two more. Then Chris threw a quickie over the line of scrimmage. Ken Morris caught it and was tackled on the spot.

Fourth and two.

"Hold that line!" shouted the Astrojet fans. "Hold that line!"

From the Vulcans came the cry, "Goal! Goal! Goal!"

Then silence as Chris barked signals. He caught the snap, faded back, passed. It was knocked down.

"He should've run with it!" cried Bucky.

"Okay, defense!" yelled Doug. "Get in there! And get back that ball!"

They got the ball back all right. And they kept it for quite a while, too. But not long enough. Time ran out, and the game went to the Astrojets, 13–7.

"We should've won it," said Jim disappointedly. "We were better than they were. Lots better."

They were riding home. Jim's mom was in

the front seat with his dad, Karen in back with Doug and Jim.

"It might have helped if you hadn't turned into stone every time you intercepted a pass," said Doug softly.

Jim stiffened. Mom looked over her shoulder. Her eyes were hurt. "Now, Doug."

"I'm sorry," said Doug. "I should've saved that till we were on the field."

"That's okay," said Jim, looking out of the window at the houses but not really seeing them. "You're right. I do turn to stone."

"You do not!" Karen cried. "And you played a good game!"

"Of course you did, Jim," Mom said. "You played fine."

"Don't get sore at Doug, Jim," Dad added, looking at Jim's reflection in the rearview mirror. "He said it because he wants to see where you can improve. He didn't say it to hurt you or humiliate you."

"For crying out loud, who's sore?" Jim cried angrily. *Boy!* He was glad when they finally got home.

He was eating supper when the phone rang. "Jim, this is Bucky. Got a minute?"

"I'm eating," said Jim.

"Okay. Come over when you finish. Got something to show you."

"Okay," said Jim. He hung up, wondering: What did Bucky want to show him, anyway?

8

Bucky opened the large, black scrapbook. Printed in white ink on the inside cover was the inscription: *This scrapbook belongs to William G. Hayes.*

"Bill has kept this up since he was a freshman in high school," Bucky explained proudly. "Didn't Doug keep a scrapbook?"

Jim flipped through the pages and saw that the scrapbook contained only pictures and clippings on sports. Bill played baseball, football, and basketball and participated in track. He was quite an athlete.

"Yes, Doug's got a sports scrapbook. But I

think he started it when he was a junior. Is this what you wanted to show me?"

"Well — not exactly." Bucky sat back in the chair while Jim read a caption under a picture of Bill in football uniform. Bill's right foot was high in the air, as if he had just kicked a football. "Lancey High's scrappy halfback, Bill Hayes, will be a key man in the game against Beacon City tomorrow afternoon," he read.

Bucky looked directly at him. "Did Doug ever say anything to you?"

Jim frowned and pulled the scrapbook off the table and onto his lap. "Say what? For crying out loud, Bucky, what're you so mysterious about? If you have something to tell me, tell me, will you?"

Bucky took a deep breath and let it out. He took the scrapbook, flipped some pages, stopped at one near the middle, and placed the book on Jim's lap. "Does Doug have that clipping in his scrapbook?" he asked, pointing at the newspaper write-up on the left side.

"Inexperienced receivers cause of loss," Jim read aloud.

You can blame inexperience of receivers in the Lancey Bobcats' 30 to 7 crushing defeat Saturday night at Croton in front of a capacity crowd.

Coach Stan Wilbur's high hopes for linebacker Doug Nardi, a sophomore, have failed to materialize. Nardi is fast, has large hands, and can catch a football like a veteran. But put an opponent near him when he does, and zowie! He'll drop the ball.

The fear of being tackled is nothing unusual. The boy has great potential. Cappie Morse, former All-American linebacker now with the Bears, practically froze into a statue every time he intercepted a pass. He almost quit, but his coach had faith in him. He liked everything else Cappie did. It took Cappie a year to get over it.

Doug Nardi will get over it, too. Let's hope he won't get discouraged and quit.

Jim felt a ball lodge in his throat. He glanced over the news item again, then looked at Bucky. "No," he said huskily. "Doug doesn't have that clipping. I know he doesn't. I've read his scrapbook a dozen times."

Bucky grinned. He took the scrapbook and flipped it to a page near the end. "Here. Read this," he said.

LANCEY BOBCAT STAR
MAKES ALL-STATE

Doug Nardi, brilliant end for the Lancey High Bobcats, was selected All-State end by a committee of coaches and sportswriters. Doug, a senior, had scored the highest number of receptions in the Tri-County School League and scored the second highest number of touchdowns.

Jim didn't read any further. This one was familiar.

"Doug's got this one," he said, smiling. "Well, why not? I'd save a clipping like that myself!" Then he frowned. "Why did you want me to read that other one, Bucky?"

Bucky shrugged. "Well, I just thought it might make you feel better if you knew that you're not the only one who ever got scared of being tackled. And who knows? You might turn out like Doug! You might even become a pro!"

Jim laughed. "Not me," he said. "Never."

But he felt better. He had never known that about Doug. Doug had never said anything about his fear of being tackled.

No wonder Doug's been easy with me,

reflected Jim. He knows what it's like to be scared, and he wants to help me without hurting my feelings.

He rose from the chair. "I'm going, Bucky," he said. "Thanks a lot."

"That's okay," said Bucky.

Jim didn't tell anyone at home about the clipping. Maybe he never would. It wasn't important to anyone else, anyway. Only to him.

All week long, except Friday, Coach Doug Nardi drilled his offense on off-tackle, end-around, and pass plays, and Bill Clark drilled the defense.

"C'mon, Ben! Pick up your feet one at a time and move 'em!" Doug would shout to the skinny left end. And to right guard Roger Lacey, "You're not posing for a picture, Rog! Move at the snap!"

Jim Nardi wasn't overlooked, either.

"You're looking for daylight, Jim! That's a fullback's job! Tear through! Get after the ballcarrier! Bring 'im down!"

They played the Saturns on the North Field on Saturday. A strong west wind swept thick clusters of clouds across the sky, and a threat of rain hung in the air. But it didn't rain, nor did the threat of rain keep the crowd away.

The Saturns, who wore blue uniforms with white stripes and white numbers, had won a game and lost a game, while the Vulcans had two losses behind them.

The Vulcans won the toss and chose to receive. For most of the first quarter, neither team could get deep into the other's territory, and the fullbacks kept busy punting. The punts were usually short for the Vulcans, usually long for the Saturns, for the wind was in their favor.

At last the exchange of punts gave the

Saturns an edge. They had pushed the Vulcans back to their own six-yard line. Chris faded back to pass and was smeared in the end zone, giving the Saturns a safety. Two points.

In the second quarter, Chris took a poor snap from center Terry Nabors. He fumbled trying to hand it off to Ronnie Holmes. A Saturn picked it up and galloped down an open field for a touchdown. The try for point missed. The half ended with the Saturns leading 8–0.

In the third quarter, the Vulcans' short passes to the ends picked up three to six yards each time. Then, from the twenty-two, Ronnie bolted through a wide open hole at left tackle and went all the way. He tried for the conversion and made it. Eight to seven.

The teams played a tight game up to within the last minute of the fourth quarter.

The Vulcans were facing the wind, just as they had when the game started. The second half had started with the Saturns facing the wind. They had had their choice of receiving or choosing a goal.

It was Vulcans' ball on the Saturns' eighteen. First and ten.

"Take Ken's place!" Doug ordered Yak Lee. "And tell Chris to keep it on the ground!" Yak ran in, and Ken Morris ran out.

They gained nine yards in three tries.

"Tell Chris to have Ronnie boot one between the uprights!" ordered Doug. Ken raced in as Yak raced out.

And that's exactly what Ronnie did, kicked one between the uprights. A field goal. The Vulcans won their first game 10–8.

Jim went to church on Sunday morning, then got his model airplane, paint, paint thinner, and brush and went into the garage.

It was a windy day. So windy you hated to step outdoors. Fortunately, the wind blew from the south and wasn't bitterly cold. That, though, was the only good thing you could say for it.

Jim played most of yesterday's football game all over again in his mind. He hadn't contributed much to winning it, but he was glad he hadn't done anything bad, either. He had had no chances for interceptions, so there had been no chance for him to freeze into a statue. Heck, people went to see statues in museums, not on a football field!

Suddenly the door opened and the wind rushed in. As Jim turned quickly to see who was there, his hand struck the can of paint thinner. The liquid splashed on the heater and *Boom!* It exploded into a giant whitish flash, and Jim went crashing to the floor.

"Jim!" someone yelled in a high, shrill voice behind him.

Close the door!" shouted Jim.

The wind was fierce. Chuckie Gorman had all he could do to shut the door.

Jim felt a searing pain on his right arm and saw that the sleeve of his sweater was on fire. He slapped at it with his other hand and put it out. Then he struggled to his feet and stared at the flames that were nibbling at the bench and chewing hungrily at the window curtain.

Terror seized him. Should he call the fire department? But the fire might spread before they got here! He looked at Chuckie.

Chuckie's face was white and his eyes big as golf balls.

"Stay there, Chuckie!" he ordered. "Don't come any closer!"

He looked around frantically and saw a water pail. But what good was an empty water pail? A long bamboo rod stood in the corner. It had been there ever since his mom and dad had purchased their living room rug.

He glanced at the burning curtains. They were beyond saving, but the fire could start on the wood. And a good start would get the garage blazing in no time.

Jim grabbed the bamboo rod and with it yanked the curtains off their hooks and pulled them to the floor. The fire had already started on the wood. Blue and orange tongues of flame were licking fiercely at the casing above the window.

"Jim! Shall I go for help?" yelled Chuckie.

"No! Don't open that door! The wind will make it worse!"

Jim rushed to the heater and turned it off. The fire was spreading on the bench. If he had on a coat instead of a sweater —

The tent! The tent they took camping every summer.

He looked up. There it was, folded, directly above his head, lying across two joists. He got it down with the bamboo rod and spread it over the burning curtains. A few seconds later, he removed it. The fire was out. He flung the tent over the burning bench, stamped it flat, then looked for something with which to smother the flames eating away at the window casing.

"Here, use my hat!" offered Chuckie. "It's leather!"

"Thanks, Chuckie!" Jim took the hat, climbed on the bench, and swatted at the flames as if they were flies. The flames flickered, then died, leaving only black, scorched wood. Jim coughed from the smoke that was filling the garage. Then he jumped off the bench, tossed Chuckie back his hat, and lifted the tent.

"Well, the fire's out!" he cried, wiping his smarting eyes. "But I've got to clear out this darn smoke!"

He started for the door, but Chuckie spun the wheelchair and opened it for him. The wind whistled in, and the smoke swirled out. Jim pushed the burnt curtains into a pile and carried them out to the trash can. Mr. and Mrs. Nardi, Doug, and Karen came rushing down the sidewalk from the back porch.

"Jim! What happened?" Mr. Nardi yelled frantically.

"A fire," answered Jim, his voice calm but his heart still pounding. "It's out, though. But we'll have to buy new curtains."

Mr. Nardi removed the cover of the trash can, and Jim pushed in the ruined curtains.

"Know what we need, Dad? A fire extinguisher. I wouldn't have had any trouble if we'd had a fire extinguisher in the garage."

He had to explain how it all happened. But Chuckie took the blame. He said the fire wouldn't have started if he hadn't come into the garage. Jim said no. That if he hadn't been careless, he wouldn't have tipped over the can of paint thinner.

Jim's dad settled it by saying, "Never mind. Just thank God neither of you got hurt and you got the fire under control."

The model plane's right wing and a tail piece had broken. But he could repair that, Jim thought.

"Look!" Mrs. Nardi suddenly exclaimed, grabbing Jim's arm. "Your sleeve's burned right through! You must have burned your arm, Jim!"

"Let's see it," said Doug. He pulled the sleeve gently up over Jim's elbow, then unbuttoned the cuff and rolled up the shirt-sleeve. There was a large angry-looking burn a couple of inches above the wrist. And, man, was it sore.

"Let's go into the house and put something on it," advised Doug. "You'd better not practice football for a week. Give this a chance to heal."

Jim stared at his brother. He started to say something, but didn't. He knew it wouldn't do any good.

Jim didn't go to practice on Monday or Tuesday. He told only Bucky Hayes why he couldn't practice. But by Tuesday noon it seemed that everyone in school had heard about the fire and his burned arm.

"How bad is it?" asked Hook Wheeler during the lunch hour.

"It's bandaged now," replied Jim. "You can't see it."

"Chuckie said it was pretty bad," said Dil. "He was there when the fire started and saw it all."

"I believe it," said Hook, looking hard at Dil. "I didn't say I didn't believe it, did I?"

He brushed by Dil and walked away, his hands stuck into his pockets. Dil looked after him a bit, then turned to Jim. "I don't know why I keep being friends with that guy. He's got a head as hard as nails. Would you believe he thinks you're faking?"

Jim frowned. "He does?"

"Sure, he does. He told me so this morning. He says that little burn is only your excuse not to play."

Jim bit down on his lower lip. "He's a punk," he said. "Hook's a darn punk."

Dil grinned. "Don't let him hear you say that."

"I don't care if he hears me or not," replied Jim. "You can even tell him what I said if you want to. I've had enough of him, anyway." He spun around, then went and sat in the gym, alone and miserable. Darn that Hook. And darn football. He wished he had never started playing the game.

On Wednesday afternoon he showed up at the field in his football gear. The guys, and Doug, looked at him in surprise.

"Thought I told you not to come to practice this week," said Doug.

"I feel okay and my arm's okay," replied Jim seriously. "I can practice."

"I gave you an order," said Doug in a stone-hard voice. "If you want to keep that uniform on, okay. But just run around the field. Handle the ball once or mix with the guys, and you're off the squad."

Jim stared at his brother. Doug's eyes were like steel, and Jim knew that he meant every word he said.

He ran around the field three times, then trotted home. He went to the field again on

Thursday. He didn't wear his uniform, only his sweatshirt. He ran around the field ten times, then, without changing his pace, ran all the way home.

On Saturday he asked Doug if he could put on his uniform. "When I said a week, I meant a week. If you wear that uniform, don't expect to play," said Doug emphatically.

Jim eyed his brother. The newspaper clipping about Doug's early football days in high school flashed through his mind, and he felt an urge to taunt Doug about it. But that was a coward's move if there ever was one. He'd never do that.

At last he shrugged. "Okay," he said. "But can I practice next week?"

"Sure. Starting Monday."

The Vulcans played the Cadets on the South Field. The Cadets had a perfect win record so far, having beaten the Vulcans once already, as well as the Saturns and the Astrojets.

Within three minutes after kickoff, the Cadets scored a touchdown on a twenty-two-yard pass, then converted. Before the quarter was over, they scored again, this time failing on the conversion try.

Jim, sitting on the bench near where Chuckie Gorman, Chuckie's parents, and his own parents were seated in the stands, watched the game with a sick feeling in his heart. There had been times when he wished he hadn't started to play football because of his fear of being tackled. But now he realized that his desire to play was stronger than ever. It hurt to sit here on the bench and be a spectator. It hurt to know he couldn't go into today's game even if he were the Vulcans' star player.

He was sore. Real sore. Doug at least let him put on a uniform and sit on the bench.

But thinking about it, what good was it to sit on the bench in football gear if he couldn't play?

Still, the desire to play stayed with him. He wanted to prove to Doug and everybody else that he was no longer afraid of being tackled. That if he had a chance of intercepting a pass, he would, even if the entire opposing team came flying at him. The desire kept building up inside him. He became nervous and fidgety.

The Cadets scored again in the second quarter and converted to lead the Vulcans 20–0.

Then Chris Howe uncorked a long pass to Pete Witz. Pete caught it in the left corner pocket and went over for the team's first touchdown. Jim rose in his seat, whistled, and yelled. He yelled louder than anyone else. Those who sat near him cheered along with him. They didn't know that this was what he needed — that he was letting out all that built-up steam.

Ronnie Holmes booted the extra point. In the third quarter, Ronnie broke through right tackle for a gain that put the Vulcans on the Cadets' nine-yard line. On the next play, Ronnie took the handoff from Chris, faked a run to the right, and handed off to right end Pete Witz. Pete bolted around left end for a yard gain.

Chris tried a pass. It was intercepted! The man was downed almost on the spot. The Cadets moved down the field like a steam-roller till they crossed the goal line for another touchdown. The try for point was good, and they led 27–7.

Chris scored on a quarterback sneak in the fourth quarter, and Ronnie kicked the extra point. But that was all the Vulcans could do. The Cadets captured their fourth game in a row to take top spot in the league.

"Well, no one can blame *you* for our losing today," said Chuckie as Jim walked alongside the wheelchair being pushed by Chuckie's father. "The Cadets were just on."

"We have two more games to play, and we'll win 'em," said Jim confidently. "You'll see. And I'm going to be in them. I'm going to be in them every minute I can."

11

Jim practiced with the squad on Monday. During scrimmage he wished a pass would be thrown to some receiver near him so he could test himself. He wasn't worried a bit about his burned arm. His mom had put ointment and a clean bandage on it. He felt brand-new again.

He didn't get a chance to intercept a pass. Doug praised him though on breaking through the line and bringing down the ball-carrier. "Just running last week seems to have done you good, Jim," he said. "You've picked up speed."

"Know what happened?" broke in Bucky Hayes. "He skidded on a banana peel and got banana oil on his knee joints."

Doug chuckled. "Pardon me for that *peel* of laughter," he punned. "Okay, let's try a couple more plays. Then run around the field twice and we'll call it quits."

Practice proceeded normally on Tuesday and Wednesday. On Thursday Jim's wish was answered. Chris Howe, quarterbacking for the offense, faded back a few steps after the snap from center and pulled back his arm. Jim, starting through the line, saw the move and stopped. He looked to his right. No man was waiting for a short pass there, but the left end was running deep. Jim looked to his left. The right end was racing down toward the corner pocket. But another man, Ronnie Holmes, was button-hooking in!

Chris lobbed a pass. Jim sprang. He

leaped high and caught the ball. As he came down with it, he saw Ronnie diving at him. He gripped the ball hard, shut his eyes, and braced himself.

And then Ronnie hit him. The blow felt like an explosion. He went down, still gripping the ball, with Ronnie's arm like a vice around his waist. He lay there a moment, then opened his eyes. Ronnie got off him.

"You lucky stiff," he muttered.

Jim fixed a smile on his face. He tossed the ball up to Doug and climbed to his feet. He had done it. He had intercepted a pass, was tackled, and still had hung on to the ball. Sure he had gotten scared. Sure he had almost fallen to pieces. But he hadn't. He had made it.

He was in the lineup Saturday. The Vulcans were playing the Astrojets, who had won two games and lost two. They were steamed up for another win. The Cadets had first place cinched, but second place was still open.

Ronnie Holmes and Tom Willis, the teams' captains for today's game, were on the middle of the field. They watched the referee toss the coin. They looked at it on the ground. Then the ref put his hand on Ronnie's shoulder, indicating that Ronnie had won the toss. The ref said something to Willis, then trotted to the thirty-yard line and spotted the football on end while the two captains ran off the field to their respective teams. A moment later, the Vulcans' offensive unit ran out to the north side of the field and the Astrojets' defensive unit ran out to the south side of the field.

The whistle shrilled. The Astrojets kicked off. The ball sailed end over end to the Vulcans' nineteen. Mike Ritter, the left halfback, took it and galloped for sixteen yards before he was pulled down.

"Let's win this for Christopher Columbus," said Bucky, huddled in his poncho against the nippy October air.

Jim frowned. "Why for him?"

"It's the twelfth," replied Bucky. "Columbus Day — the day he landed in the New World."

"Boy! Are you a whiz at history!" said Jim, giving his friend a shove with his elbow.

The Vulcans kept the ball on the ground for their first three plays and gained eight yards. Then Ronnie plowed through center for three, picking up a first down.

On the first play, Chris Howe faked a handoff to Mike, then flipped a lateral to Ken Morris, who was running behind him from his right halfback position. Ken took the pitch and bolted around left end.

Ronnie swept in to throw a block on the right linebacker, and Ken raced to the Astrojets' twenty-four before he was tackled.

The Vulcan fans roared, and Bucky slapped Jim heartily on the back. "Another first down! That was a hot play, man!"

Ronnie bucked, but lost two yards on the play. Mike took a handoff and started a long spurt around right end. The Astrojets' left line broke through and chased Mike back. He started toward the opposite side of the field, saw two linebackers swooping at him, and started back the other way.

"Oh, no!" yelled Hook Wheeler, standing at Jim's left side. "Run forward, you nit! Not backward!"

"Please, somebody, tackle him before he goes into our end zone!" wailed Jim.

Mike was hit on the Vulcans' thirty-five and was brought down on the thirty-four.

"Good thing that Astrojet wasn't thinking," said Jim. "He might've scared Mike all the way back to the goalposts."

Third and thirty-two. Now was the time they needed another hot play. Chris took the snap and faded back. His arm came around. The ball left his fingers and whipped through the air in a perfect spiral. It sailed over the head and uplifted arms of an Astrojet safety man and into Ben Trainor's waiting arms.

Ben pulled the ball to his chest and raced down the field. The safety man gained on him inch by inch, and caught up with him on the six. Chris bucked for three, then Ronnie plunged over for the touchdown.

"Man, are we hot today!" cried Bucky.

"Chris Columbus will be happy," said Jim with a smile.

Ronnie kicked for the extra point. It was good. Seven to nothing.

The defense went in, and the offense came out. "Hold 'em, Jim!" a familiar cry rose from the right side of the stands. Jim waved. I'm going to try, Chuckie! he said to himself.

Hook Wheeler kicked off. The ball sailed through the air, barely turning. An Astrojet back caught it on the twenty-one and got good blocking as he brought it back up to the thirty-eight. On the first play, Jim bolted after a man who was on the verge of throwing a block on Marv Wallace, who in turn was within two yards of the ballcarrier.

Jim struck the Astrojet from behind. A flag went down. A couple of seconds later, Marv tackled the runner. The man went down on the Vulcans' thirty-one.

The whistle shrilled. Jim, climbing to his feet, saw two flags on the ground and frowned. The ref and an umpire were discussing something. Then the umpire trotted away, and the ref signaled the clipping motion and pointed at the Vulcans.

"That was you, in case you didn't know," Hook Wheeler said to Jim. "Clipping."

"Me?"

"Who else? Don't you know you can't jump on a guy from behind unless he's carrying the ball?"

The ref stepped off fifteen yards from where the runner was tackled and spotted the ball on the Vulcans' sixteen. The Astrojets got into a huddle, then broke out of it and went into formation at the line of scrimmage. Tom Willis barked signals.

"Hup one! Hup two!"

The snap. Willis faded back and lobbed a pass over the scrimmage line to the right. Jim saw it coming and sprang for it. It was a wobbly pass. It struck his fingers and bounced to the side. He grappled for it, and in his hurry and fear of losing it, he knocked the ball clumsily to the ground.

Oh, no! he thought despairingly. Oh, no! He fell to one knee, his head drooping.

12

Second and ten. Astrojets' ball.

I've got to make up for that muff, thought Jim. I've got to. The guys must think I dropped the ball because I was scared. I wasn't scared. The ball wobbled too much.

Willis called signals, then took the snap and faded back. Jim drove hard through the line. He kept his head down, just high enough to see the quarterback's waist. His padded shoulders thudded against other padded shoulders as he plowed between the center and tackle and barely missed stepping on Marv Wallace, who had fallen to his knees.

And then, barely a yard from Willis, Jim dove. He hit the quarterback solidly and knocked him to the ground.

"Hey!" the quarterback shouted.

Jim, lying on top of Willis, knew instantly that something was wrong. Willis was glaring at him. His arms were outflung on the ground.

Jim rose bewilderedly to his feet and saw the ref standing only a foot away. At his feet was a red flag.

Where was the ball? What had happened, anyway?

Then he saw an Astrojet throw the ball from the sidelines and then, and only then, did he realize what had happened. Willis had thrown a pass.

"Yak," Jim addressed the right linebacker, "what happened? They get a touchdown?"

"No. The pass was thrown out of bounds. But you fouled. You nailed Willis *after* he had thrown the pass."

"What a booboo, man," said Hook, throwing him an icy glare above the bar of his face mask. "That ball was already out of bounds when you hit Willis. Didn't you see him throw it?"

Jim, dazed, stared at him. "That's a stupid question, isn't it? I wouldn't have tackled him if I had."

"I wonder," said Hook.

The ref counted off fifteen yards and spotted the ball on the one-yard line.

"Why don't we just give 'em the touchdown and start all over?" Hook grunted disgustedly.

"Don't be a sour apple all your life," rapped Bucky Hayes. "Jim's in the middle of every play. Every time that ball is snapped, he's either busting through the line to get at the ballcarrier or knocking down a pass. All you do is wait back there for a pass or for some runner who makes it past the linebackers. Maybe that pass would've been good and it would've gone for a touchdown if Jim hadn't busted in like he did. Maybe he scared Willis into throwing the pass wild. Have you thought about that? No. All you're looking for is an excuse every time to knock Jim. What've you got against him, anyway?"

"Nothing," said Hook, his eyes like slits cut in white paper. "Who said I've got anything against him?"

"Then cool it," replied Bucky. "And don't —"

"Okay, Buck," interrupted Jim, nudging his arm. "I think you've said enough." And, thanks, he wanted to say. Thanks for popping off to Big Mouth.

The teams lined up at the line of scrimmage. The Vulcans formed a tight wall as they faced the Astrojets. Jim and the other linebackers stood close behind them, the safety men a few yards back.

The snap. Helmets clattered and shoulder pads thudded as both lines belted each other. The whistle pierced the air. The struggle halted. The men unpiled.

"They didn't make it," someone shouted.

The Vulcan fans roared, grew silent again.

The ref spotted the ball in the same place.

"GOAL! GOAL! GOAL!" screamed the Astrojet fans.

They quieted. The teams lined up. The quarterback barked signals. There was the snap. And again the pileup.

"We held 'em!" cried Bucky.

The Astrojets had gained a foot. Only two feet to go. Third and goal.

The lineup. The snap. Willis faded back

two steps and passed. Ben Trainor leaped in front of the intended receiver. And batted down the ball!

"Way to go, Ben!" yelled Jim, thumping him on the back.

Fourth and goal.

"Hold 'em, men! *Hold 'em!*"

The snap. Willis bucked on a sneak. Jim plowed forward to stop the quarterback from reaching the goal line. All his effort was concentrated on this last drive.

The men unpiled. Willis was on the ground, the ball was under his head, and his head was six inches from the goal line. "He didn't make it!" the Vulcans yelled enthusiastically. *"He didn't make it!"*

They jumped, danced, shouted. It was the Vulcans' ball now. On their six-inch line! The defense ran off the field; the offense ran on.

"We stopped 'em for you guys!" cried Bucky. "Move it up!"

Ronnie Holmes plowed through for three yards, Ken Morris for two, then Chris snapped a pass to Ben Trainor. Ben caught it and was down on the fourteen. A first down!

They moved the ball to the twenty-eight when the horn signaled the end of the quarter.

Jim sat on the bench, his helmet in his hands. He felt good, but not too good. He still hadn't made up for that lousy mistake. The guys might still think he was scared of being tackled. Except Bucky, maybe. But Bucky was a pal.

13

The Vulcans reached the Astrojets' eighteen, then lost the ball on a fumble.

Willis clicked with a thirty-two-yard pass to his right end, but an Astrojet guard was offside, so the ball was taken back. The half ended with the Vulcans leading 7–0.

Within a minute from the start of the second half, the Astrojet quarterback pulled a sneak and took off on a run that netted him forty-four yards. Two plays later, he threw a touchdown pass. A try for the point was good, and the score was tied at 7–7.

In the fourth quarter, Ronnie Holmes broke through right tackle for a twenty-one-yard run. He rammed through the same spot for another six-yard gain. Then Chris Howe tossed a pass to Ben Trainor in the corner pocket. Ben caught it and galloped down an open field to a touchdown. Ronnie booted for the extra point. It was good, and the game ended with the Vulcans on the fat end, 14–7.

"Bucky," said Jim as they were walking home, "thanks for telling Hook off. But maybe you shouldn't have. Maybe you've made an enemy."

"No loss," replied Bucky. "He's just a big blowhard, anyway. Let's just forget it. We've got enough to think about with next week's game with the Saturns coming up. Just think — it's our last game of the season."

"And it's also our last chance to win second place in the league," Jim replied grimly.

"One! Two! Three!"

Rip Kiley, the Saturns' quarterback, caught the snap from center and faded back. Jim Nardi started through the narrow gap between center and left tackle. The center fell in front of him, stopping him momentarily. Jim got up and struggled forward. At the same time, Rip lateraled the ball to his left halfback. The halfback started toward his right side of the line, then saw Jim coming and reversed his run.

Jim chased him toward the left side of the line. There he and right linebacker Yak Lee tackled the runner for a two-yard loss.

"Jim, what would you have done if you were that runner?" asked Bucky.

"What d'you mean?"

"Well, you and Yak came at him like a couple of tanks."

"Oh." Jim shrugged. He knew what Bucky meant, all right. "I don't know," he said finally. "Guess I'd do what he did. I'd go down."

Bucky laughed. "Yeah! Guess you would, wouldn't you?"

The Saturns' ball was on their thirty-one. Second and twelve. No score and less than four minutes to go in the first quarter.

The snap from center. Rip Kiley faded back. He tossed a short one over the left side of the line. Jim saw it coming, but the play was too far away. The Saturn end caught it and was smeared almost on the spot by Yak Lee. A gain of four yards.

Third and eight. Another pass. A long

one. Jim halted inches away from Rip, turned, and saw the ball spiraling beautifully through the air. A glimmer of hope welled in him as he saw Hook Wheeler coming up under the ball. Catch it, Hook! Catch it!

Hook leaped. He caught it! Or did he? Jim saw a blue-uniformed player behind him, saw him sprint down the field, Hook chasing after him. Hook couldn't catch up. The Saturn went over for a touchdown. Seconds later they converted. Seven to nothing.

In the second quarter, the Saturns' burly fullback broke through a hole in the line and scampered down the field for a fifty-nine-yard run. Two plays later, they got their second touchdown. Then converted. Fourteen to nothing.

"That Chuckie's got guts," said Bucky

thoughtfully. "He came in his wheelchair, but he's yelling like everybody else."

Guts, thought Jim. The will to do something above all odds and not give up. He had read that somewhere. Chuckie had it, all right.

Ken Morris took the kickoff and ran it back to the Vulcans' thirty-three. Chris Howe handed off to Ronnie Holmes, and the fullback galloped to the thirty-nine. On the next play, right tackle Marv Wallace was offside and the ref placed the ball back on the thirty-four.

"Nice going, Marv," grumbled Bucky.

Chris tried to pass. It was incomplete. Then Ronnie booted a punt that hit the twenty-yard stripe and bounced out of bounds.

"Hold 'em, Jim!" yelled a familiar voice as Jim pulled on his helmet and started out on the field.

The Vulcans' defense held the Saturns from scoring, but when the offense took the field, the Saturns' powerful defense held them, too. The half ended with the score still 14–0 in the Saturns' favor.

Go team, go!" yelled the Vulcan fans as the teams ran onto the field to start the second half. The fifteen-minute break had given the Vulcans time to rest, time to regain some of their much-needed stamina. They felt fresh, eager, and ready to go.

The Saturns kicked off. Mike Ritter caught the ball and carried it almost to mid-field in a dodging, twisting, galloping run.

In three plays, the Vulcans gained a first down, putting them in Saturn territory. A long pass to Ben Trainor was complete and down on the Saturns' fourteen. Then Chris fumbled and a Saturn landed on the ball.

"Shucks!" grunted Bucky, running onto the field with Jim. "Thought we were heading for a touchdown!"

"Let's get the ball back from 'em."

"Gee!" Bucky said, grinning, flashing white teeth behind the bars of his face mask. "Who would've thought of that but you!"

Rip Kiley tried a pass. It was incomplete. He tried another, a short one over center. Jim saw it spiraling toward a Saturn, button-hooking in from his left side. He sprinted in that direction, leaped, and caught the ball! As he came down with it, he saw the Saturn dive at him. A paralyzing fear suddenly took hold of him — the same fear he had felt several times before when he had intercepted a pass.

Hang on! he told himself. Hang on!

He not only hung on — he stiff-armed the

Saturn, broke through the pile of tackles and guards to the left, and sprinted down the field! A safety man charged at him. He shifted the ball to his left arm, stiff-armed the man, and raced on. Another Saturn was coming at him. Jim put on more speed and kept his distance ahead of the Saturn.

And then he was in the end zone. Touchdown!

The Vulcan fans stood up in the stands and shouted like crazy. "All right, Jim!"

"Beautiful, Jim! Beautiful!" yelled Doug.

Even Hook Wheeler slapped him on the back and grinned. "I take back everything, Jim! Nice play!"

"Thanks, Hook."

Hook kicked for the extra point. It was good.

The game went into the fourth quarter with the Saturns still leading 14–7. It was their ball on the Vulcans' thirty-one. First and ten. The Saturns took a handoff from Rip Kiley and plunged through tackle for eight yards, then tried the same thing and hit a cement wall.

Bucky chuckled. "We don't let 'em do things like that more than once," he said.

Third and two. The fullback tried a line buck through the other side of the line. A loss of one. Then the Saturns went into punt formation. The fullback kicked. The ball rolled into the end zone, and the ref placed it on the twenty.

The Vulcans tried a reverse and gained eleven yards. Ronnie Holmes broke off-tackle for six. Then Chris, on an option, ran for sixteen yards around right end. A long pass to Pete Witz clicked, and the score was 14–13. Ronnie kicked for the extra point.

It missed by inches!

"Lousy luck!" cried Jim, slapping his thigh resentfully.

No one was sitting on the bench. The coaches, the subs, and the defensive unit were all standing. The atmosphere was crackling with suspense.

"Get out there, you guys, and get that ball!" yelled Doug. "Come on, Hook! Buck! Jim! The old fight!"

The Saturns ran the kickoff back to their twenty-nine, only five yards from where they had caught the ball. They tried a run around left end and gained two yards.

Then Rip Kiley flipped a short pass over the line of scrimmage. It was high and looping. Was it too high? Jim leaped as high as he could and touched the ball with the tips of his fingers. It dropped, and Jim pulled it to his chest. He tore through a hole in the scrimmage line and just got past it when he saw two Saturns charging at him, one from his left side, the other from his right.

He grabbed the ball to his stomach,

lowered his head, and bolted forward. Then they hit him. Helmets and shoulder pads thumped. He felt pain in his sides and in his arms as he sagged and the men piled on him.

He heard the whistle. The Saturns climbed off him, and he lifted his head and saw the ref standing above him, reaching for the ball. He sprang to his feet and saw Bucky, Marv, Yak Lee, and Hook grinning at him.

They ran off the field and let the offense take over. In two running plays, the Vulcans advanced the ball to the Saturns' eight. Ronnie bucked for three, then two, then Chris took it over. Ronnie kicked the extra point, and the Vulcans went into the lead 20–14.

Fifty seconds later, the game was over. The Vulcans shouted and danced. Some of them tossed their helmets into the air. Then they went and shook hands with the unhappy, beaten Saturns.

"You know what?" said Hook. "I hate to see the season end. We were just gettin' started."

"I feel like that, too," said Jim. "Maybe we can get more teams in the league next year. How about it, Coach?" He smiled at his brother.

"Maybe," replied Doug. Then he smiled, too. "Little brother," he said, "you did fine. Just fine. You know, several years back, when I was playing —" He shrugged and shook his head a little. "I'll tell you about it some other time."

Jim met his eyes squarely. "You don't have to, Doug. I know all about it."

Doug frowned. He started to say something, but just then Chuckie Gorman pulled up between Doug and Jim in his wheelchair and stuck out his hand. He shook Doug's hand first and then Jim's.

"Congratulations, you guys," he said. "I knew you'd pull it off. But I was sweating it out for a while!" He looked up at Jim, and his eyes twinkled. "Coming over after supper tonight, Jim? I'll let you race the Porsche. I've got new wheels on it."

"New wheels?" cried Jim. "You bet I'll be there!"

FINAL STANDINGS

	WON	LOST
Cadets	5	1
Vulcans	3	3
Saturns	2	4
Astrojets	2	4

Matt Christopher ®

Muhammad Ali	Randy Johnson
Lance Armstrong	Michael Jordan
Kobe Bryant	Peyton and Eli Manning
Jennifer Capriati	Yao Ming
Dale Earnhardt Sr.	Shaquille O'Neal
Jeff Gordon	Albert Pujols
Ken Griffey Jr.	Jackie Robinson
Mia Hamm	Alex Rodriguez
Tony Hawk	Babe Ruth
Ichiro	Curt Schilling
LeBron James	Sammy Sosa
Derek Jeter	Tiger Woods

MATT CHRISTOPHER

Read them all!

- Baseball Flyhawk
- Baseball Turnaround
- The Basket Counts
- Body Check
- Catch That Pass!
- Catcher with a Glass Arm
- Catching Waves
- Center Court Sting
- Centerfield Ballhawk
- Challenge at Second Base
- The Comeback Challenge
- Comeback of the Home Run Kid
- Cool as Ice
- The Diamond Champs
- Dirt Bike Racer
- Dirt Bike Runaway

- Dive Right In
- Double Play at Short
- Face-Off
- Fairway Phenom
- Football Double Threat
- Football Fugitive
- Football Nightmare
- The Fox Steals Home
- Goalkeeper in Charge
- The Great Quarterback Switch
- Halfback Attack*
- The Hockey Machine
- Hot Shot
- Ice Magic
- Johnny Long Legs
- Karate Kick

*Previously published as Crackerjack Halfback

All available in paperback from Little, Brown and Company

**Previously published as Pressure Play

***Previously published as Baseball Pals